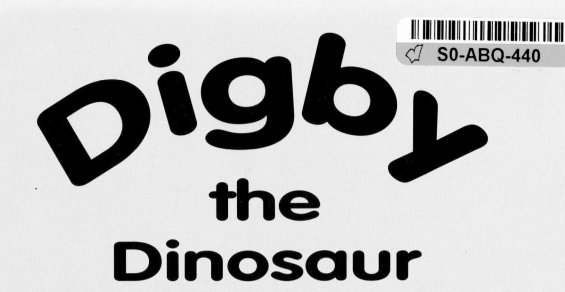

Digby
the
Dinosaur

by
Alan Aburrow-Newman
Illustrated by
Gill Guile

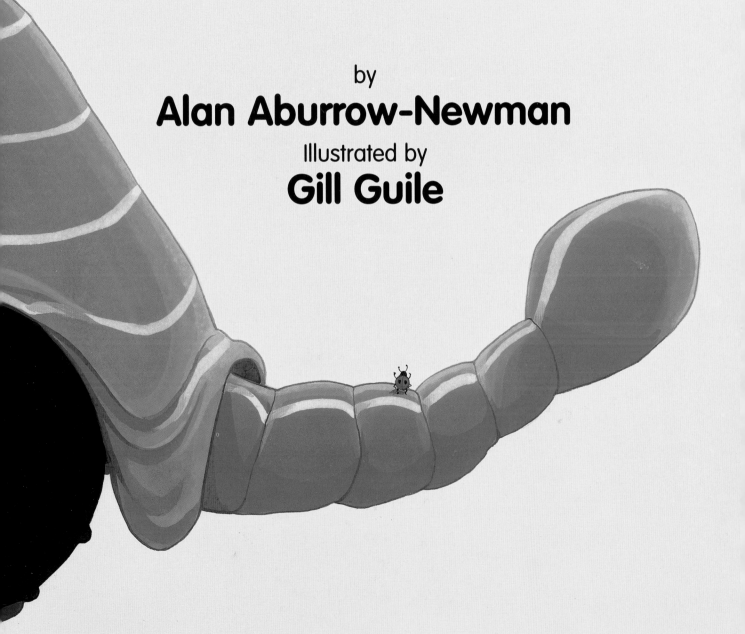

Brimax · Newmarket · England

Very early one Saturday morning, Big Bill the driver arrived at Digby's garage. Over his shoulder and around his neck was a long hose. It was coiled so high, Digby could just see the top of Big Bill's cap! He had a scrubbing brush in one hand, and a bucket filled with sponges and soap in the other. Cleaning rags stuck out of every pocket.

"We have an important job to do today," said Big Bill. "You must look as smart as the day you arrived at the garage. At the moment you look like the world's biggest mud pie!"
Digby felt nervous. He liked being muddy, and he had a horrible feeling that something wet and soapy was about to happen.

Digby had never had a bath quite like it! Buckets of water were thrown over him. He was brushed and scrubbed and squirted so hard with the hose, that lumps of mud went flying in all directions. The garage floor looked like a muddy pond. At last Digby began to look like a digger again.

"Where are we going?" asked Digby, wriggling as his tummy was squirted with water.

"If I tell you, it will spoil the surprise," said Big Bill. "And the sooner you keep still, the sooner you will find out!"

Washed and polished, Digby really did look as good as new. His bright yellow paintwork was gleaming; his glass was glittering; his wheels were the brightest yellow. "Oh! Please tell me," said Digby. "Where are we going?"

"You will just have to wait and see," said Big Bill. "Today we are going somewhere very special." Big Bill changed his boots for shiny shoes and climbed into his seat in the cab.

"Off we go then," he said happily as he started Digby's engine.

Driving through the town, Digby passed lots of places that *he* thought were special. First of all there was the lemonade factory, where he had made the new truck parking lot.

Then there was the playground, where he had put the new swings and slides.

There was the swimming pool that he had dug all on his own.

And there was the park where he had made the flower beds, and a pond with a fountain for the goldfish. But they didn't stop at any of these places.

"We are almost there now," said Big Bill. "Close your eyes and I will tell you when to open them. And make sure you don't peek!"
Digby was just about to have a quick peek, when he heard lots of children calling his name.
"Hoorah for Digby!" they were shouting.

Digby opened his eyes. He was at the school. "What am I doing here?
Am I making a new playground or helping to plant some big trees?"
"No!" shouted the children. "We are going to dress you up for the carnival!"
They were so excited, they skipped and danced around Digby until he
began to feel dizzy.

The children began dressing Digby up. They put bright green blankets over his cab and wrapped green cloth around his digging arm.

"What am I going to be in the carnival?" Digby asked Thomas, who was painting him with wiggly, yellow stripes.

"Wait and see," said Thomas.

"What are you dressing me up as?" Digby asked Harriet and Laura. They were sticking big, white cardboard teeth onto his front digging bucket.

"Stop asking questions," said Harriet.
"You are not supposed to find out until we've finished," said Laura.

"Joshua, will you tell me what I look like?" Digby said to the little boy painting two red eyes next to the big teeth.
"I can't! It's a secret!" Joshua whispered back.

"Please tell me! *Please!*" said Digby. "A secret is no fun when I am the only one who doesn't know what the secret is!"

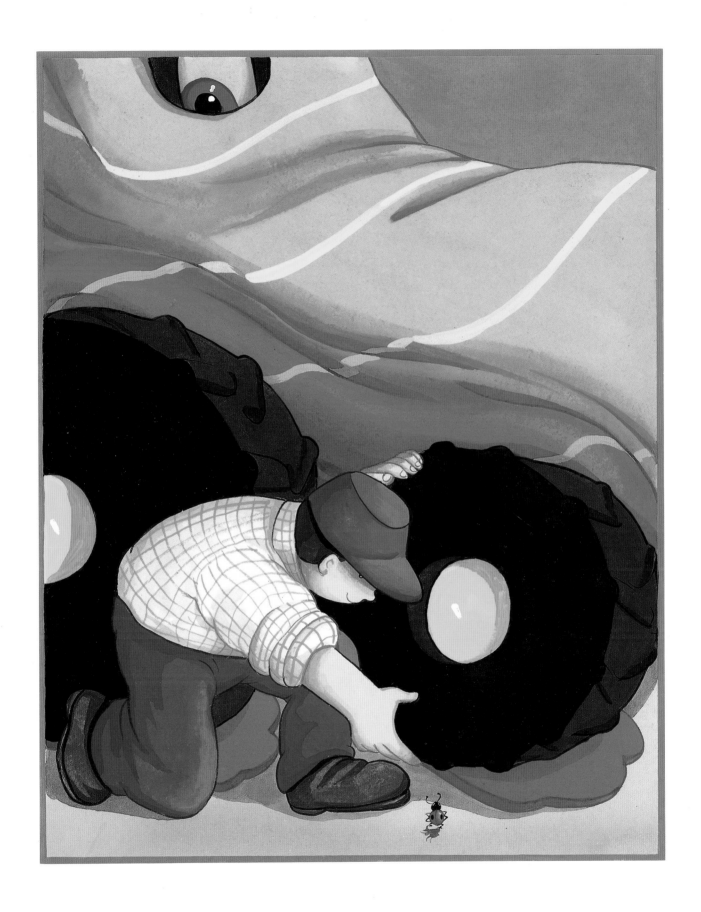

"They are nearly finished," said Big Bill. He was helping to put some big rubber feet onto Digby's wheels. "Now there is only the tail to go!"

When the children had finished wrapping and sticking and painting and fixing, they all stood in a big circle around Digby. He had never seen so many smiling faces.

"You are the biggest and best in the world," the children shouted.

"We've made you green with yellow stripes, with bright, red eyes, huge teeth, big feet and a long tail. You look at least a million years old. Guess what you are, Digby?"

Digby thought hard, but he couldn't think of a single thing that was green with yellow stripes, red eyes, huge teeth, big feet and a long tail. "I give up," he said at last. "Now PLEASE tell me what I am!"

"You are a dinosaur!" the children cried. "A huge green and yellow dinosaur!"

Digby saw his reflection in the school window. He really *did* look like a dinosaur. His front bucket was a big, square head which he could lift up as high as a house. He had a big mouth and sharp, pointed teeth. His cab was a lumpy, humpy back and he had a long, snaky tail that he could swish from side to side. The rubber feet were best of all. They slapped and flopped as his wheels went round, making noises just like a real dinosaur walking in puddles.

"I am a **diggersaurus**!" said Digby. "The strangest dinosaur of all!"